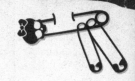

MONSTER HIGH
ADVENTURES
OF THE
GHOUL⚡SQUAD

Little, Brown and Company
Hachette Book Group
1290 Avenue of the Americas, New York, NY 10104
Visit us at LBYR.com
Visit monsterhigh.com

First Edition: December 2017

Little, Brown and Company is a division of Hachette Book Group, Inc.
The Little, Brown name and logo are trademarks of Hachette Book Group, Inc.

The publisher is not responsible for websites (or their content) that are not owned by the publisher.

Library of Congress Control Number 2017953690

ISBNs: 978-0-316-55725-2 (paperback), 978-0-316-55730-6 (paper over board), 978-0-316-55728-3 (ebook)

Printed in the United States of America

LSC-C

10 9 8 7 6 5 4 3 2 1

MONSTER ⚬ HIGH

ADVENTURES OF THE GHOUL ⚡ SQUAD

Happy Howlidays, Ghouls!
The Junior Novel

ADAPTED BY
Perdita Finn

BASED ON THE SCREENPLAY WRITTEN BY
Keith Wagner

LITTLE, BROWN AND COMPANY
New York   Boston

Chapter 1

It's a Wonderful Monster's Life

Draculaura looked up the hallway for her friends. She didn't like to walk to class alone in the morning. She saw skeletons, zombies, phantoms, and monsters of all kinds but not her special crew of ghouls. Where were they? She opened her locker, which had a mirror on the door. But she couldn't see her reflection in it. No vampire could. Thank goodness Webby, her pet spider, was there.

"All good?" she asked him, touching her hair.

He gave her four excited thumbs-ups. She looked great! Her long black hair was styled in two ponytails, showing off her hair's pink streaks to perfection. She was wearing a matching outfit with a pink shirt and a flared black skirt. She had a pink heart-shaped beauty mark on her cheek.

"Draculaura!" Clawdeen was rushing down the hallway toward her. Fluffy werewolf pups, her brothers and sisters, yipped at her heels, and she shooed them on ahead of her as she stopped to talk to Draculaura. Draculaura wondered what it was like to have such an enormous family, since it had always been just her and her dad, Dracula.

Clawdeen put down her books. She was grinning, clearly pleased with herself. She held up her hands, her fingers spread apart so they looked like the fangs of a bat. "Ready?" she asked Draculaura.

Draculaura made fangs with her fingers too. The ghouls clapped their hands together and finished by fluttering them like bats. It was the official best friends forever vampire handshake.

"Ha!" exclaimed Clawdeen. "Told you I'd get it." She'd been practicing all week.

Draculaura was thrilled. "Clawdeen, you are probably the only werewolf in the world that can do the vampire handshake." What she didn't say was that now, at least, she had someone to share it with. There weren't any other vampire ghouls at Monster High. Draculaura didn't even have a sister she could teach it to. But she did have a friend, a good ghoulfriend, a wonderful werewolf friend!

"C'mon, ghoul," Clawdeen said with a smile. "We're gonna be late for Humanology."

Just ahead, Bonesy and Skelly were hurrying to

class, each with a stack of books in their skeleton arms. Skelly was growing tired, so he plopped his books on top of Bonesy's pile. Bonesy's arms popped off and clattered to the floor along with all the books. Gob the blob monster was at the water fountain. When he finished, he ripped the entire tank out of the wall and swallowed it whole.

Draculaura smiled. Another ordinary day at Monster High.

Chapter 2

The Spooky Spirit of the Season

A large vampire bat fluttered past the students to the front of the classroom. With a twist of his black wings, he turned into Dracula. Draculaura's dad was also a teacher at Monster High—and the founding headmaster. "All right, everyone," he announced in his deep voice. It was time for Humanology to begin, where monsters learned all about the strange and mysterious world of humans.

A white sheet covered a table at the front of the room. Monsters pointed at it and whispered.

Dracula cleared his throat as a few last monsters hurried in, including Draculaura and Clawdeen. Gob squished in after them, leaving a trail of water behind him. Dracula sighed. Gob had probably eaten the water fountain again. "Take your seats," he told the late arrivals. "It's time to learn all about…" He paused dramatically, his hand on the sheet just before whipping it off. "…human holidays!"

On the table was the strangest assortment of weird and wonderful objects. Balloons, a box with a bow on it, a huge family dinner, and a pumpkin with a face carved into its front. What could all this possibly mean? What were holidays, anyway? The students pointed and whispered.

Clawdeen was already writing in her notebook. Draculaura peered at the table, eager for an explanation.

"Human holidays," lectured Dracula, "are special days throughout the year that humans have deemed worthy of celebration." He picked up the box with the bow on it. "This is a present." He wrote the word on the board, and students copied it into their notebooks. "It is something you give to somebody else as a way of saying, 'Hey, I think you're pretty fangtastic.'"

He passed it to Abbey, who was sitting in the front of the room. The abominable snow monster turned it over in her hands, frowning. "It looks like box," she said in her thick accent.

"I just love boxes," purred Toralei the werecat, stretching her claws.

"The present is inside the box," explained Dracula. "You have to open it."

"How can you open it if it's wrapped up in all that paper?" Frankie Stein asked. She was holding the box now and passed it to Clawdeen. When their hands touched, Clawdeen felt the tingle of a shock. Frankie was extra electrical today.

Dracula laughed. "You tear the paper off! Then you open it."

Clawdeen shook her head. Humans were just so weird. "Well, why wrap it up in paper in the first place if you're just gonna rip it all off?"

Dracula cleared his throat. Students sat with their pens poised above their notebooks. "Well, I…" he began. He cleared his throat again. He scratched his chin, stalling for time and thinking. "Because humans are weird, that's why! Moving on! Another human holiday tradition is the big family meal." He looked around on the table. Nothing was left on it except the balloons and the pumpkin. "There was a big family meal here. Where did it go?"

Gob burped. Crammed into the giant goo of his belly were a turkey, a few bowls, and a candelabra, its candles still lit. He blushed when Dracula shook his head. He hadn't thought anyone would notice.

"Mr. Dad?" Draculaura asked. "This is all very interesting, but I'm curious. Why do the humans have these holidays?"

"Why?" He scratched his head. The students had so many questions today. "Well," he began, "because… because…" He flipped through some notes he had on his desk.

Abbey shrugged. "Who knows? Why does stomach howl like werewolf when yak milk gone sour? Just another of life's great mysteries."

Her classmates stared at her, bewildered.

"What?" she said, raising an eyebrow. "Not happen to you guys?"

"I am sure," announced Dracula authoritatively,

"that we could come up with hundreds of theories as to why humans have holidays. But the fact is, without actually talking to a human, we'll never really know."

Students scribbled in their notebooks. But Draculaura still wasn't satisfied. Who would she give a present to, she wondered. And why? Why didn't monsters have holidays?

"Now," Dracula continued. "Next up we have…" He turned to the table, but there was nothing on it anymore. No balloons. No pumpkin. Nothing. "Gob! Are you serious?"

The monster had gobbled up everything. He covered his face with his squishy hands and giggled. The pumpkin was yummy.

Dracula shook his head. Teaching young monsters really wasn't the easiest job in the world.

Chapter 3

The Mapalogue Express!

Later that night, alone in her room, Draculaura couldn't stop thinking about the present. Her dad had let her take it to her room to study. Webby, hanging from a thread beside her, was studying it too. He rubbed his chin thoughtfully.

"Oh, Webby," Draculaura said with a sigh. "There must be a good reason for all of this."

Maybe all she needed to do was *see* a human holiday in action for herself. Maybe then she'd understand what all the fuss was about.

The Monster Mapalogue was for finding monsters. It could locate any monster in the world. All you had to do was say the name of the monster, and it would teleport you right to where that monster was. Draculaura had used it to locate most of the students who now lived and studied at Monster High. But tonight Draculaura wasn't going to go looking for monsters. She wanted to find humans…humans having a holiday!

Webby was holding the present and shaking it when she sat down beside him. "I wonder..." she said. She put her hands on the Monster Mapalogue. Would it go somewhere where there were no monsters? What if the only thing she knew was the place itself? It was worth a try. *"Normie Town…Exsto monstrum."*

Nothing happened.

"That figures." Draculaura sighed. "I guess that I'll never—"

But before she could say another word, Draculaura was gone!

Chapter 4

You Better Watch Out!

Draculaura looked around, stunned. There was a neat row of human-style houses in front of her. A streetlight shone in the night. "I'm in Normie Town!" she exclaimed. The Mapalogue had done the trick.

She crept over to one of the houses, where she heard sounds of laughter. Very carefully, she peeked in through a window. It looked like nothing she had ever seen. There was a tree in the middle of the room covered in lights and sparkling orbs. There were red socks hanging over a fireplace—and there were tons of boxes with bows under the tree. Presents! Not only was she in Normie Town, but the humans were clearly having a holiday.

They were all sitting on chairs in a circle near the tree. They were laughing. In the middle of the circle, a little girl was holding out her hands in front of her and lurching forward. The humans would shout out words, and the little girl would shake her head no.

"*Raaa!*" shouted the girl.

"You're a grizzly bear!" guessed an older human man. *Probably the girl's dad,* thought Draculaura.

"A polar bear!" added an older human woman. *Probably the girl's mom.*

"Some kind of bear," said a little boy. With a pang, Draculaura realized this was probably the little girl's brother. It must be fun to have siblings and share games together.

"No." The girl giggled, shaking her head again. "I'm a monster!"

"Again?" asked her father. "You already did *monster!*"

"Well, you didn't get it last time, either." The girl giggled again.

Despite herself, Draculaura laughed too. The little girl's expression was so cute and funny.

The human father looked up, concerned. "Did you hear that?"

Yikes! Draculaura covered her mouth with both hands.

"Maybe it's a real monster!" said the little girl from inside the house. Her eyes sparkled with excitement.

"Honey, we talked about this," her mother answered. "There's no such thing as monsters."

But the little girl wasn't listening. She was already out the front door and circling around the yard toward the window where Draculaura was hiding.

Draculaura scooped up the Mapalogue and ducked behind a tree just in time. But the little girl was smart, and she was headed right toward the tree. She jumped around to the back of the trunk to catch the hidden monster. "Gotcha!" she shouted.

But no one was there. The little girl frowned. She looked around. Nothing but shadows.

What she didn't see perched on a branch above her was the tiny bat, clutching the Mapalogue. Only when the human girl was back inside did Draculaura let herself change back into a ghoul.

"Pretty sure it was a monster," the little girl told her family when she was back inside.

Her mother smiled, amused. "Oh? And what did the monster look like?"

The little girl held up her hands and began staggering around, roaring. The whole family laughed, and Draculaura, peering through the window again, wanted to laugh too. There was some special magic about this holiday that just made her feel happy. But she was very quiet. She had to be. That was a close call after all. She'd better get back to Monster High as fast as possible. But she didn't want to leave. She wished she could stay and see what the family did next.

Only much later when she was back at Monster High and tucked into her bed did she wonder about what she had learned. What were the humans doing, anyway? She kept thinking about the mother and the father, and the little human girl and the little human boy. It must be nice to have a whole family who was just like you.

Chapter 5

The Howliday Countdown Begins

The next day before class, Draculaura told her ghoulfriends about everything she'd seen. She felt as though she'd discovered something—an important clue—but she didn't know what it was. Maybe they would help her figure it out. Clawdeen, Lagoona, Frankie, and Cleo were all clustered around Draculaura's locker.

"So," said Cleo, skeptical. "You're saying human holidays are about stomping around and growling?"

"Well, hey! I can do that," Clawdeen said with a laugh. She tossed her wild mane of hair and growled.

"No!" Draculaura shook her head. "What I mean is, well, it's about family. And friends. And laughing. And just being with one another."

Clawdeen looked at her, confused. "Well, we can do that too."

Draculaura's face lit up. Of course they could! "Which is why," she announced, "we are going to create the first monster holiday. A *howl*iday!"

"That's a voltageous idea!" Frankie exclaimed. "If the humans get to have holidays, why can't we?"

"I love it," agreed Lagoona. "But what do we do on our howliday?"

Cleo pulled out a notebook and began scribbling. "Pyramids, of course. Great, big decorative pyramids. It's not an occasion without them. I can picture them now." She pursed her lips, thinking. "We'll have elegant mummy wrappings draped from the rafters—and then I can come riding in on a giant golden Sphinx!"

She turned her notebook around so all the other ghouls could see what she had drawn. It showed Cleo on top of a big cat with a pyramid in the background. It was a nice picture and all, but it didn't look like what Draculaura had seen the humans doing.

"Cleo," said Clawdeen gently. "Your howliday sounds a little...mummy-centric."

Cleo grinned. "I know! And see how happy I look!"

Draculaura stepped in. "*This* holiday is going to be for all monsters."

"But we have vampires, werewolves...and whatever Gob is," said Frankie with concern. "How do we come up with something that makes everyone happy?"

Draculaura thought for a moment. "I say we ask the students what they think the howliday should be about." She noticed Cleo was busily tapping on her phone. "You're already pricing giant golden Sphinxes, aren't you?"

"You never know," Cleo said with a shrug, "what the other students are going to want. We might as well be prepared."

Chatting about how best to call a school meeting, the ghouls headed to class. But Draculaura hung back. Cleo had her sister and Clawdeen had a whole pack of siblings, but Draculaura's only family was her father. She kept thinking about the family she'd seen laughing together the night before. The ghouls could come up with a plan for a howliday, create decorations and wrap up boxes, and give presents to one another. But how did you celebrate a howliday when you didn't feel like you have a whole family?

"You coming, ghoul?" called Clawdeen. She held up her hands to make bat fangs.

Draculaura smiled and mirrored her friend's fingers. The girls clapped their hands together and waved them in the air. What was she thinking? She had the best ghoulfriends in the whole world, and they were her family—and they were going to make the best howliday ever.

Chapter 6

A Rumor of Vampires from Howlidays Past

"**D**raculaura! Clawdeen!" called Frankie as the ghouls arrived in class. "Over here—we saved you a spot."

Frankie had disconnected her hand from her body and draped it across two seats right next to her. The hand flashed the ghouls a thumbs-up as they hurried over. Draculaura reattached it once they were seated.

"All right, students, settle down," Dracula announced. "I trust you did the reading assignment on prominent vampire families throughout history."

Rayth, who was a particularly good-looking wraith, stuck his hand in the air. "Um, Mr. Dracula? I couldn't do the reading because I accidentally took Deuce's history book by mistake."

Deuce, sitting beside him, nodded. The snakes that made up Deuce's gorgon hair hissed in agreement. "Same here. 'Cause I took Rayth's book."

The gorgon and the wraith exchanged pleased looks and high-fived each other. They swapped their identical history books. Dracula stared at them, confused. He'd missed something.

Ignoring the boys, he continued. "Those of you who did do the reading should be all up to speed about the history of the royal Van Bat family." He clicked on a projector, and a painting of an old-fashioned vampire family filled the screen at the front of the room. They looked stuffy and royal. They all wore dark capes, and their dark hair was slicked back in an unstylish fashion.

"I can't imagine what it must have been like to be part of such a powerful family," Lagoona whispered to Cleo.

Cleo turned up her nose. "Speaking as a royal heiress myself, I can tell you, it's pretty great. People do whatever you want. If you want a Sphinx for the howlidays, they give you a Sphinx for the howlidays. Just saying."

Draculaura's hand was in the air. She had a burning question. Why had her father never told her about this family before? "Dad? Um, Mr. Dracula. Vampires live for thousands of years. Wouldn't that mean members of the Van Bat family might still be out there somewhere?"

"A good question, Draculaura!" exclaimed her father. And one he could answer with confidence. "The Van Bat family all but vanished when humans arrived in Transylvania."

Clawdeen looked up from the history book, which she had been reading. "What about those rumors about the secret Van Bat princess?"

Dracula sighed. "I believe they were just that. Rumors. If there were a Van Bat princess living in Transylvania, I'm sure we would know about it."

"But what if the rumor is true?" Draculaura was feeling excited. "What if she's out there? All alone? Like I was before we started Monster High. Maybe we could use the Monster Mapalogue to go find her. If there is a Van Bat princess out there, she deserves to know that she's welcome here at Monster High."

Dracula gazed indulgently at his daughter. "I appreciate your concern, Draculaura. But even if there is a princess, we don't know her first name. Without the full name of a monster, the Mapalogue won't be able to find her."

Draculaura opened her mouth and then shut it again. After all, just last night the Mapalogue had taken her to the humans having a holiday. She didn't know *their* names, but still it had found them. But if she told her father that she had been to Normie Town and risked detection, he would be very angry with her.

"Now," Dracula was continuing. "Let's move on to notable ghosts and phantoms in the late sixteenth century. Page five hundred sixty-five in your textbooks."

The students all flipped their textbooks open to the right page—except for Deuce and Rayth.

Rayth squinted. "Ah, nope, nope," he said at last. "Deuce, this is actually *your* history book."

Rayth and Deuce switched textbooks again. Dracula sighed. Teaching monsters really was a lot of work.

Chapter 7

Bah! Humbug! Dangerween!

The ghouls met in the auditorium at the end of the day. They'd called a school meeting, and everyone showed up. The ghouls were sitting on a stage behind a table like judges. Draculaura got up to address the audience.

"Hello, everyone!" she called. "And thank you all for coming to pitch your ideas for the new monster howliday!"

"Don't be shy!" Lagoona spoke up. "Remember, there's no such thing as a bad idea."

Cleo brought her hand down on a buzzer. *Bzzz!* "But in case that's not true," she explained, "I brought this bad-idea buzzer." *Bzzz!* She made it buzz again.

Clawdeen took the microphone. "First up, we have Rayth and Deuce!"

Deuce Gorgon ambled onto the stage, grinning. The snakes in his hair hissed. "Okay, check it out," said Deuce, his hands in his pockets, relaxed. "Rayth and I came up with a howliday called Dangerween."

Frankie gulped. "It sounds dangerous."

At that moment, Rayth zoomed onstage wearing a turbo-powered jet pack—and, thankfully, a helmet. "Oh, it is dangerous! So dangerous!" he shouted.

Cleo's hand reached for her buzzer, but Draculaura stopped her. She smiled politely at the boys. "Next!" she called and waved them off the stage.

Abbey wheeled a giant wagon onto the stage. On top of it was a giant block of ice. She stood beside it in her furry white boots and stared at the audience without moving. Everyone waited.

Eventually, Clawdeen spoke up. "I'm confused," she admitted.

"Is ice," said Abbey matter-of-factly.

"Right," said Draculaura.

"Ice make everything better," explained Abbey.

Cleo sighed audibly. "But what does it do for the howliday?"

"Nothing." Abbey's expression didn't change. She just stood there. "Ice is ice," she said last. "So, what do I win?"

Cleo's hand reached for the buzzer. Again, Draculaura stopped her.

"Next!" called Frankie. "Here comes Gob to

demonstrate a howliday he calls Gobsgiving!"

Beep! Beep! Beep! A garbage truck slowly backed up onto the stage. It was loaded with all kinds of food—roasts and casseroles, pies and potato salads, and fancy cakes of all kinds. Gob wobbled out of the truck, a bib around his neck and his mouth open wide.

Cleo reached for the buzzer immediately. Draculaura slid it away from her.

When they had finally gotten Gob back and the truck off the stage, Gil Webber, a river monster, pushed out an enormous water tank in front of the audience. Gil got inside it. Once he was completely submerged, he began to explain his howliday. But all anyone could hear was, *"Glub, glub, glub."*

Cleo was looking more and more irritated. She kept checking her phone. Frankie was trying to keep a smile on her face but looking more and more hopeless. Even Lagoona, who seemed to be perpetually cheerful, was looking glum. Draculaura couldn't hide her disappointment at all. She thought of the decorated tree she had seen and the family laughing around it. The sparkling lights and the light of their laughter had all been part of the magic. What were they missing about holidays? Something. Something important.

Another ghoul had taken the stage, disguised in dark glasses and a hat. But the mummy wrappings on her legs gave her away. She was giving a slide show presentation. "Great, big decorative pyramids," she began.

"Cleo!" shouted her friends.

"Yeah, all right," Cleo admitted, and turned off the projector. The ghouls had agreed to keep their own ideas to themselves so everyone else in the school could have a chance to share theirs.

Toralei pushed Cleo aside as she came to present her idea. She didn't have any props or costumes. She took the microphone and addressed her classmates in the sweetest of voices. "I think the howliday should be all about getting together with your family."

Draculaura looked up, surprised. *Yes!* This is what

she had been thinking. Exactly. A holiday wasn't about decorations but about how you spent time with the people you loved. It was about family and togetherness.

Toralei's whiskers twitched. "And you should spend the whole day bickering and arguing with them!"

"Why do I have to do this every single year?!" meowed one of her sisters, appearing from the stage wings.

"Can I go now?" yowled another sister.

Toralei screeched at the top of her lungs, baring her teeth and hissing at them.

Abbey peeked around from behind the curtain. "Just checking if you wanted to see ice again."

Draculaura exchanged a look with Clawdeen. This was a disaster.

At the end of the presentations, the ghouls had no idea what to do next. As the monsters filed out of the auditorium, the ghouls began to talk about what they'd seen.

"Everyone gave us so many howlidays. How are we supposed to choose?" Clawdeen wondered out loud.

Lagoona perked up. "What about Gil's howliday? That seemed fun. Spend all day underwater! Anyone?"

Frankie was flipping through her notes and sighing. "Boo Year's Eve, Saint Batty's Day, Bring Your Spider to Work Day..."

Webby peeked up over the edge of the table and gave everyone four thumbs-ups. He liked that idea!

Draculaura smiled at him. "They're all so creative," she said kindly. "But I don't see a howliday that's going to make every kind of monster happy." In truth, she didn't even see the kind of howliday that was going to make *her* happy.

Chapter 8

The More the Merrier

That night, alone in her bedroom, Draculaura couldn't sleep. She stared up at the ceiling, wide awake. Webby was snoozing in a hammock he'd spun for himself, but when Draculaura got out of bed, he opened his eyes.

"*Shh!*" whispered Draculaura.

Webby held up eight fingers to his own mouth in response. "*Shhhh!*" he whispered.

Draculaura turned on the light at her desk. She took out her history book and began flipping through it. Holidays were about families. Toralei was right, even if her family couldn't stop fighting with one another. And while Draculaura didn't even have siblings or cousins to invite to a howliday, it made her much sadder to think of the lost Van Bat princess, who didn't have anyone at all.

She pulled the Mapalogue close. It was glowing.

She took a deep breath. She was about to lay her hands on it when a shadow loomed over her.

It was her father! He closed the Mapalogue. "Where do you think you're teleporting at this time of night?" he demanded to know.

Draculaura batted her eyes innocently. "To the Creepateria?" she tried. "For a glass of water? Teleporting is so much faster than walking. All those stairs…"

Dracula was not amused. He narrowed his eyes sternly. He could always spot a lie—at least when Draculaura was telling it.

"I was going to look for the Van Bat princess," Draculaura confessed.

"And how did you expect to find her?" Her father shook his head. "The Mapalogue won't work without her first name."

"Not true!" Draculaura blurted out. "I figured out that if you know—you know—a few things—about where you want to go," she stammered, trying to cover, "like if she's a vampire and she's a princess, the Mapalogue will teleport me someplace that's close to a vampire princess."

"Someplace close?" That wasn't good enough for Dracula.

"Close-ish," revised Draculaura.

"In other words, you have no idea where you are going."

"Not a clue, no," Draculaura admitted.

Dracula pulled up a chair and sat down beside his daughter. Really, if being a teacher was hard, being a father was even harder. "You are my daughter, the fright of my life," he told her. "And I simply cannot allow you to go out teleporting to mystery locations all by yourself."

He kissed her on the top of her head, picked up the Mapalogue, and turned to leave.

After he was gone, Draculaura grinned. He'd given her exactly what she needed. She could follow his rules and still go search for the Van Bat princess. The only thing she had to do? Not go by herself! It would be better to go with friends, anyway.

Chapter 9

'Tis the Season for a Monster Mission

The rest of the ghouls couldn't wait to go looking for the vampire princess. Once she'd gathered all her friends, Draculaura knew there was only one more thing she needed—her father's permission. She found him in the library studying a big, dusty book. All the ghouls gathered around his desk.

"What is this?" he asked, suspicious. "What are the smiles?"

Draculaura took a big breath. "You said I couldn't go look for the Van Bat princess alone. Well, as you can see, I'm not alone anymore!" She turned to her friends. "Do that smile thing again."

All the ghouls grinned broadly.

Dracula shook his head, but before he could speak Draculaura was making her case.

"Dad," she began, "this is a team of the most talented, special ghouls I know. Frankie's got the brains. Lagoona's amazingly athletic, and Clawdeen is fierce and determined."

"And I am all of those things," interrupted Cleo. "Besides being an actual princess myself."

"Dad, do you remember what unlife was like before we created Monster High?" Draculaura continued.

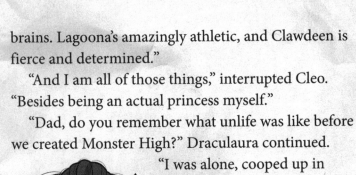

"I was alone, cooped up in my room with no other monsters to turn to. But now we have a place to call our own. If there is a vampire princess, then she's probably just like I used to be. And she deserves to be told there's a whole school of monsters waiting to welcome her home."

"She's good," Cleo whispered to the other ghouls. Dracula was quiet, considering what his daughter had said. "Do you ghouls promise to look out for one another?"

They all nodded.

"*Yes?*" shouted Draculaura.

"*Yes!*" shouted all the ghouls.

"Do you promise to wear helmets and life jackets and sunscreen when appropriate?"

"*Yes!*" shouted all the ghouls in unison.

Dracula looked from one ghoul to the next. Sometimes being a parent meant letting your little monsters grow up. "You can go," he said at last.

The ghouls cheered.

"But," he interrupted them, "first, we do research."

Their faces fell.

"*Awwww,*" moaned Lagoona.

"Hey," Dracula warned them. "I just said you can go. Be excited about the research."

"Yay, research." Lagoona sighed.

"Yay," echoed all the others in tiny, unenthusiastic voices.

Dracula collected books, scrolls, and old notebooks of his own research for the ghouls to read, and they met to study together. Everything was piled up on a table in the library, and the ghouls stared at it, overwhelmed.

"I have assembled everything we know about the royal Van Bat family," Dracula explained. "Where they lived. Family history. Last known whereabouts."

Frankie flipped through a file dossier. "So organized," she said politely. "And it's got that new binder smell."

The other ghouls stared at her in disbelief.

"What? I like binders," protested Frankie.

Dracula nodded appreciatively at her. "The Van Bats lived in Transylvania for centuries," he lectured. "So that's likely where the Mapalogue will take you. But remember, you could find yourselves anywhere, so stay alert. Any questions?"

"Yes," Cleo spoke up. "Does rescuing a lost vampire princess count as extra credit? Because my average in Mad Science class could really use a little love."

Dracula stared at her without answering. Really. The questions these monsters asked!

"You're in charge of this," he said, handing the Mapalogue over to Draculaura.

Draculaura flipped it on. It began to whir and glow. The ghouls all reached out their hands and touched it.

Draculaura met their eyes and grinned. Now they were ready for the fun part at last! She was ready to speak the magic words. *"Van Bat...Lost Princess. Exsto monstrum!"*

An instant later, they were gone.

Chapter 10

Deck the Halls with Dust and Cobwebs

It was the middle of the night, and the only light was the glow of the moon. Mountains loomed in the distance. The ghouls stood in the middle of a bare field looking around. It was creepy, spooky, and totes fangtastic.

Draculaura knew exactly where they were. Transylvania! "We made it!" she exclaimed. "That means there must be a Van Bat princess."

Frankie did not look relieved. "But we have no way of knowing how far away she is. Or which direction to start looking."

Cleo pointed toward the edge of the mountains. "How about the big, creepy vampire castle over there."

Out of nowhere a jagged bolt of lightning cut across the night sky. A wolf howled. It was Clawdeen. "That's a start!" she said, pleased.

When they reached the front door of the ancient

castle, Draculaura grabbed ahold of its heavy knocker at once, bringing it down again and again. *Bang, bang, bang.*

"*Hellooo!*" howled Clawdeen. "Princess Van Bat?"

"We've come all the way from Monster High to find out if you're real or just a rumor!" Draculaura called out by way of explanation.

But there was no answer. Draculaura put her ear up to the door, but she couldn't hear anything—no answering call, no footsteps, no sound at all.

Cleo, her hands on her hips, shouted toward one of the upper-story windows. "If you're not real, please let us know when to stop looking!"

Draculaura tried to open the door, but it was stuck tight.

"Wait a minute!" Frankie had noticed something. "This castle definitely belonged to the Van Bats. Look!"

The ghouls crowded around.

"What are we looking at?" asked Clawdeen.

"There on the door," Frankie pointed. "That's the Van Bat family crest. Or part of it, anyway."

The ghouls looked at the faded crest, blankly.

Frankie shook her head. "It was in Mr. Dracula's research. Didn't you ghouls read it?"

"I skimmed it," said Cleo defensively.

Frankie held up her finger, and it began to spark. She traced around the crest, filling in the missing details with a charred marking. Now the girls could see what she was talking about. But something even more surprising happened when the outline was complete—the whole crest began to glow! An instant later, the door to the castle swung open. They'd cracked the secret code.

"Dad was right!" said Draculaura. "It *was* a good idea to do some research before we left. Thanks, Dad!"

Draculaura peeked into the dark and gloomy front hall. Frankie grabbed a torch from a sconce on the stone wall and zapped it until it began to burn, sending a flickering light across the room. Cobwebs hung from the rafters. The old furniture was covered in dusty sheets.

"Look at this place!" Lagoona exclaimed. "It's like going back in time to a different century."

Clawdeen ran her finger along a line of thick dust. "I dunno, Draculaura. It doesn't look like anyone's lived here for years. Except maybe for those guys up there."

A few bats fluttered up near the ceiling.

"But the Van Bats lived here at some point," protested Draculaura. "Spread out and look around. Maybe we'll find a clue about where they've gone."

The ghouls began exploring the room's wide expanse. Cleo headed over to an antique couch and was just about to sit down when she noticed an open box covered in brown paper. It wasn't covered in cobwebs and dust—and it had a recent postmark on the outside. She peered inside and pulled out...a purse. A very stylish purse.

"Hey, ghouls?" she called. "Take a look at this." She held it up.

"That bag totally goes with what you're wearing Cleo, but is now really the time to be accessorizing?" asked Clawdeen.

"This bag is from last season," noted Cleo. "I know because I have five. Which means..."

"Somebody does live here," Draculaura finished, excited.

But Cleo never heard her answer. She was gone!

"Gahh!" Cleo screamed. A trap door had opened up right underneath her feet, and she'd disappeared down a long slide.

"Cleo!" called all the ghouls together. They peered into the blackness trying to see where she had gone.

"We have to figure out where it goes!" Frankie cried.

"It goes outside," answered Cleo, pulling cobwebs out of her hair as she reappeared though the front door. "It's a slide that sent me back outside of the castle. Keep your eyes peeled for more trap do—"

She was gone. Again! Another trap door had opened up under her feet. A moment later, she marched through the front door. This time she was irritated. "Okay, that's enough," she announced.

The ghouls looked around cautiously. Every step might be booby-trapped!

"They're everywhere," said Lagoona. She put her foot lightly on the floor as a trap door opened up underneath it. But she backflipped away from it before it could send her sliding outside. "Let's get to the stairs, mates!" she called.

The ghouls took off running as fast as they could across the hall as trap doors opened up everywhere. Clawdeen turned into a wolf for extra speed and power. Draculaura turned into a bat. Lagoona flipped this way and that way toward the main staircase.

Frankie's foot slipped underneath her, and she was just about to disappear out of sight when Lagoona reached out a hand, grabbed her, and swung her to safety. Draculaura and Clawdeen transformed back to normal and tried to catch their breath.

"Someone clearly does not want us to be here," said Frankie.

"Makes no sense," Cleo disagreed with her. "I'm welcome everywhere I go."

Clawdeen was studying a painting on the wall

Clawdeen was studying a painting on the wall across from them. It showed a little vampire ghoul in an old-fashioned dress with petticoats and a lace collar. She was wearing a cape and had long dark hair. "*Hmm,*" she wondered to herself. "Could this be the ghoul we're looking for?" She looked up at the bats above them, hanging upside down…and staring right at them. Suddenly, she had an idea.

Grinning, she turned to Draculaura. "Let's do that vampire handshake one more time," she suggested.

"Right now?"

"Trust me," Clawdeen said. She held up her fingers and made fangs.

Draculaura held up her fingers as well. The girls clapped their hands together and began fluttering them like bats. As they finished, Clawdeen noticed a bat that had been staring at them had spread its wings and was swooping right toward them!

Just as she had thought! The bat transformed into a little ghoul. She looked just like the vampire in the painting—only her clothes were more up-to-date and so was her hairstyle. She had pink ears that poked up through her dark, wavy hair. She had tiny little fangs that peeked out over her lips.

"Only vampires know that handshake," said the ghoul, surprised. "How do you know how to do that?"

Clawdeen wrapped an arm around Draculaura. "Because my best ghoulfriend is a vampire."

The ghoul's eyes widened in surprise. "Wait." She turned to Draculaura. "You're friends with a werewolf? How is that possible?"

"That's how things are at Monster High," explained Draculaura. She was used to how confused monsters could be when she first told them about the school. What she wasn't used to was talking to another vampire—especially one as cute and sweet looking as this ghoul.

"What's Monster High?" asked the little vampire.

"Imagine a place where all different kinds of

monsters and ghouls are together under one roof," Frankie told her.

"Everyone is welcome at Monster High," added Lagoona.

"And we have a pretty decent Taco Tuesday in the Creepateria," said Cleo.

The ghoul looked at the monsters sitting on her steps. She looked around the gloomy hall. "I've been hiding here all by myself for so long," she admitted. "But Monster High sounds like a place I would very much like to go."

Draculaura beamed at her, delighted. She was totes adorable. When she'd imagined another vampire at Monster High, she'd always thought about a ghoul to hang out with her and her friends, a teenage ghoul. But somehow this was even more special, even though she wasn't sure exactly why. She couldn't wait to introduce her to everyone—especially her dad.

"Sorry about the whole dropping-you-down-trap-doors thing," the little ghoul apologized.

"No problem!"

"Don't worry about it!"

"I fall through trap doors all the time," added Cleo kindly. After all, this little ghoul was royalty.

"They were very clever," Draculaura complimented her.

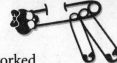

"They were?" The ghoul was pleased. "I worked really hard designing them and figuring out exactly where people would step if they came through the front door."

"You got that down," admitted Cleo.

The little vampire ghoul was standing on her tiptoes. She seemed excited. "All right then. My name is Fangelica—and I'm ready to go to Monster High."

Draculaura pulled out the Monster Mapalogue. *"Monster High. Exsto monstrum!"*

Chapter 11

The Nightmare Before Dangerween

The ghouls landed on their feet on the balcony overlooking the main hall of the school. Beneath them was total chaos.

Ghouls were shouting at one another, monsters were fighting, and no one was getting along with anyone else. Gob was pushing a wheelbarrow piled up with layered birthday cakes and holiday pies. Gil was sulking in his water tank, refusing to come out. Abbey had blocked the hallway with an even bigger block of ice than the one she had wheeled onstage during the assembly about the howlidays. Toralei's claws were out, and she and her sisters were chasing one another in circles, screeching at the top of their lungs.

"What's happening?" gasped Clawdeen.

Rayth and Deuce flew over to them, wearing jet packs.

"We got tired of waiting for you to make a decision

about the howliday," answered Rayth. "So everyone decided to just go ahead and have their own howliday by themselves."

"Dangerween!" screamed Deuce, blasting past the ghouls. Rayth jetted after him.

"Will everyone keep it down?" screeched Toralei. "We can barely hear ourselves bickering!"

Draculaura frowned, upset. This was not how she wanted to introduce Monster High to Fangelica. The ghoul was overwhelmed. Her eyes were wide, and she'd covered her ears with her hands.

"Monsters are very loud," she said.

"Happy Howlidays?" tried Clawdeen.

"What's a howliday?" Fangelica asked in a quiet voice.

"It's when friends and family get together to celebrate and enjoy one another and laugh together and give presents."

Fangelica's happy face fell. "But I don't have any friends or family."

A crash interrupted them. Rayth wasn't looking where he was going and knocked into Gob's wheelbarrow. It teetered and was about to fall on top of him.

"Gob!" called Clawdeen. She leaped from the balcony and transformed into a wolf in midair.

She dashed across the hallway, grabbed Gob with her teeth in the nick of time, and hurled him to safety before the tower of food came crashing down. Gob slammed into Abbey's block of ice, which careened down the corridor toward another group of students.

Frankie grabbed the Mapalogue. *"Abbey Bominable. Exsto monstrum."* She teleported next to Abbey on the ice block. *"Draculaura. Exsto monstrum."* Frankie and Abbey vanished together back onto the balcony as the ice block slammed into Gil's water tank and shattered into slivers of icicles.

But the diving tank sprang a leak and cracked open, sending a tidal wave of water down the hall. Everything was out of control. Lagoona dove from the balcony into the rising waters, rescuing monsters.

"Quick! Change!" Draculaura told Fangelica, and the two ghouls turned into bats and fluttered up over the chaos.

Lagoona paused, looking around. "Is that everyone?" She was depositing a water-logged student onto a floating island of Gob's treats.

"No!" shrieked Toralei. She was terrified of water. She hated getting her paws wet. Lagoona scooped her up and deposited her on the raft of food.

The waters rushed out the front doors of the school. But just as it was beginning to look like things might return to normal, a giant golden Sphinx crashed into the hallway.

"Cleo!" shouted the ghouls. They had told her not to order it!

The monsters on the food island were swept out the front door. Lagoona swam after them. The bats followed. What a disaster.

"You ruined my howliday!" yelled Gil.

"This is all your fault!"

"What were you thinking?"

"Dangerween? Seriously?"

"I thought you said all the different monsters got along with one another at Monster High," Fangelica said to Draculaura. They had turned back into ghouls.

"They do." Draculaura sighed. "Just not about the howliday."

"But I thought howlidays were about friends…"

Tears welled up in Draculaura's eyes. "This howliday was supposed to bring everyone together. But it's tearing the school apart."

Toralei shook herself dry beside them. "Toldya this is what the holidays are all about."

"No!" protested Draculaura. "I'll show you what the holidays are about…"

She had an idea. She took Fangelica by the hand and grabbed the Mapalogue from Frankie. "Try to gather everyone in the library," she told her.

She had to prove to Fangelica that at Monster High everyone knew how to work together. Besides, she had more reason than ever to celebrate a howliday because, for the first time ever, there was another vampire ghoul to share it with. She looked down protectively at the little ghoul holding her hand.

Chapter 12

Hooray for All Monsters' Day

By the time the students were all gathered in the library, they were quieter—and drier. A large computer screen had been set up so everyone could see it. After everyone was seated, Draculaura appeared on the screen, with Fangelica beside her. She was in Normie Town—right next to the house where she had first seen the holiday. She was using her iCoffin to send a video message. All eyes were on her.

Draculaura cleared her throat. "When I first wanted to have a holiday for monsters, I had no idea what it would look like. But it doesn't matter what we actually do during our howliday. As long as we have this."

She walked over to the window of the house and held up her phone so everyone could see what was happening inside the house. The family was sitting around their tree again, laughing together. They were wrapping presents and talking with one another.

The lights inside glittered and sparkled.

The students were mesmerized. It was hard to explain, but it made each feel mysteriously happy.

"There's, uh, a lot more laughter and togetherness," noticed Deuce. "And a lot less arguing and jet packs going on over there."

Embarrassed, Rayth turned to Gob. "Sorry our howliday messed up your howliday, Gob."

Abbey nodded tersely to Gil. "And I am sorry your howliday was too weak to withstand my ice, fish boy."

"We all went a little overboard," Gil admitted. "We should just be happy to be together."

Draculaura snuck a glance at Fangelica. This was the Monster High she wanted to show her.

"Can I say something?" asked Fangelica from beside Draculaura.

"Of course," everyone said together from the library.

"You can't do everyone's howliday, but maybe you could take a little bit from each one."

Frankie's eyes were glittering. She was thinking. "Right. Like instead of crazy jet packs, we just do some simple sparklers instead?" Her fingertips began to sizzle and spark.

"And we don't need mountains of food," agreed Lagoona, staring at Gob. "But we should still have a meal together."

"And instead of a really big Sphinx, maybe just a kinda big one," said Cleo.

"That's the spirit!" Draculaura exclaimed. "This is going to be a howliday for all monsters! And that's why we should call it—" But she wasn't looking where she was going, and she crashed into the trash can again. *Clunk! Thunk!*

Inside the human house, the little girl looked up, startled. "Mom! I heard it again! The monster came back!"

Draculaura grabbed Fangelica's hand and teleported back to the library as fast as she could. The screen went dark.

Draculaura caught her breath. "I think we should call it All Monsters' Day."

Everyone cheered! That's what they should celebrate! The fact that they were all different but they could all get along with one another.

"Let's put it on the calendar," Frankie said at once. "The first All Monsters' Day will be this weekend!"

Everyone pulled out their iCoffins and tapped their schedules.

"Oh my ghoul," realized Clawdeen. "That's, like, in three days."

"Three days?"

"Three days!"

"We'd better get started!"

"There's not much time!"

Draculaura grinned down at Fangelica. "Ah! I love the howlidays!"

"Me too!" Fangelica agreed. "Me too."

Chapter 13

Monsters in Floatland

The monsters were going to have a parade on All Monsters' Day—and that let everyone create their own float and express their creativity and their pride in their own special way.

Rayth, Deuce, Skelly, and Bonesy were going full rock-and-roll. They were setting up giant speakers on a platform and plugging in their amps. Venus McFlytrap was watering a border of pots on her float. Huge vines were already growing out of them and beginning to bloom. The ghoulfriends were making a giant papier-mâché replica of the Mapalogue. After all, it was what had helped them find most of the monsters in the first place.

Lagoona was having a blast. "What a creeperific idea, having a big parade to celebrate the first howliday. I cannot wait for All Monsters' Day." She sighed happily and put another wet, gooey strip onto the sculpture they were making.

Draculaura and Fangelica were working on the other side of the platform. "Wrench?" asked Draculaura.

"Wrench," answered Fangelica, pulling one out of the toolbox.

Dracula was peering over them, a concerned look on his face. "This is not a race. Slow down. Fangelica, stand back a little."

Fangelica took a tiny step backward. Draculaura turned the wrench ridiculously slowly.

"Maybe just a little bit slower…" Dracula suggested.

Draculaura exploded. "Dad! For the last time, I am not going to hurt myself. I've got this."

"All right, all right." He sighed. "I'll give you your space." He took a tiny step backward.

"Dad!" protested Draculaura.

"Space," he said. "Got it." He turned into a bat and hovered in the air just above them.

Draculaura's eyes met Fangelica's, and both ghouls burst into fits of the giggles. "I bet you wish you had my dad around when you were making all of those booby traps at your castle," said Draculaura jokingly, and Fangelica smiled.

Frankie, watching them, felt funny. She and

Draculaura had been the first monsters to meet each other—and they were like sisters. Was she jealous? Yes, she was, a little bit. But not of Fangelica. She was jealous of something else.

Clawdeen's ears twitched, and she stopped working. "Stop," she told the others. "You ghouls hear that?"

They all froze. What could be happening? Clawdeen's nose twitched. She was on high alert. "Nobody move," she ordered. "They're coming! They're right…over…*here!*"

Clawdeen reached her hand inside the float and pulled out a pair of yapping werewolf pups. Clawdeen pulled them close and began wrestling with them. "Think you can sneak up on your big sis? I could hear you panting a mile away!" She laughed.

She tossed them into the air and caught them, and they howled, delighted. More werepups heard the commotion and scampered over to join the fun until there was a huge, noisy dog pile right beside the float.

Frankie watched them. There was that funny jealous feeling again.

"What's wrong, Frankie?" asked Lagoona, noticing her.

"Huh?" Frankie turned around. "Nothing's wrong."

"She's lying," Cleo remarked. "Her left neck bolt always sparks when she lies."

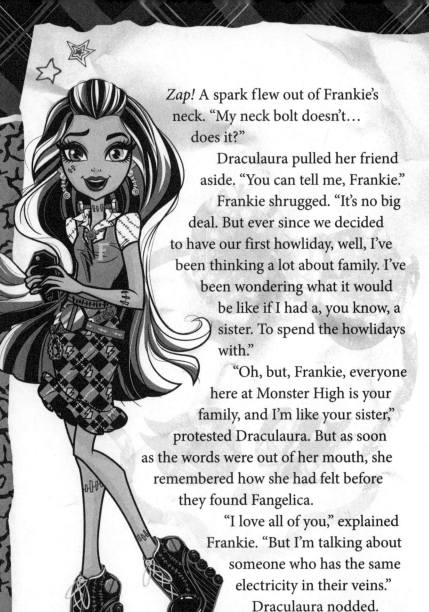

Zap! A spark flew out of Frankie's neck. "My neck bolt doesn't… does it?"

Draculaura pulled her friend aside. "You can tell me, Frankie." Frankie shrugged. "It's no big deal. But ever since we decided to have our first howliday, well, I've been thinking a lot about family. I've been wondering what it would be like if I had a, you know, a sister. To spend the howlidays with."

"Oh, but, Frankie, everyone here at Monster High is your family, and I'm like your sister," protested Draculaura. But as soon as the words were out of her mouth, she remembered how she had felt before they found Fangelica.

"I love all of you," explained Frankie. "But I'm talking about someone who has the same electricity in their veins." Draculaura nodded. She looked over to where

Fangelica was working on the float. She knew exactly what Frankie was talking about.

Frankie saw Fangelica too, and that gave her an idea. A voltageous idea! "I just thought of something," she explained. "You ghouls have this float, right?"

Draculaura nodded, and her friend raced off. She went over to help Fangelica. Her father, in bat form, was hovering again.

"Do not mind me," he insisted. "I am just an ordinary bat who is definitely not your father. Please continue."

Fangelica's eyes met Draculaura's again, and both girls giggled. He could be so silly sometimes!

Chapter 14

DIY Gift Ideas!

While everyone else was outside working on their floats, Frankie was in the science lab. She was scribbling equations on a whiteboard. "I was built in a laboratory," she said to herself, "the product of science and electricity. So who's to say I couldn't use the same process...?"

She studied her numbers. She erased one number and added another. That was it! She could do it. She could build her very own little sister. She grinned. "She'll be just like me in every way! She'll be smart. Confident. And most important, she'll love science!" They'd have secret handshakes and share sparks, and her little sister would ask her for all kinds of advice and Frankie would share with her everything she knew.

It was time to get to work. "But first," she said, picking up her iCoffin, "a little mad science music to set the mood." She tapped her phone, and the ominous sounds of organ music filled the room. Frankie wrinkled up her face. "No, that's not quite right." She tapped her phone again. A popular pop tune began to play. Frankie grinned. "There we go."

She put on her goggles and set to work. There were test tubes to fill and electrodes to plug in and wires to cross. Eventually, she picked up a giant cable and jammed it into her own neck bolts. Electricity lit up the room and sizzled through the cables and flowed toward a sheet-covered mound on an examining table. *Bzzz! Zapp! Zzzzz!* What was happening?

The sheet began to ripple. It began to rise. Something underneath it was sitting up!

"She's alive! She's *alive*! She's Alivia!" exclaimed Frankie, thrilled. "Hey, I like that. Her name is Alivia."

Frankie unplugged the cables from her neck and took off her goggles. Very carefully, she approached the sheet. She took a big breath and pulled it off. There was a brand-new ghoul, blinking her eyes and stretching. She had a frazzle of glowing yellow-and-blue hair and bright-blue lips. She was amazing. She was electric! She was Frankie's very own creation. She looked, wide-eyed, at Frankie.

The wonders of science never cease to astound and humble, Frankie thought to herself. *A moment of this magnitude deserves an eloquent statement that captures the enormity of creation. You only get one shot at this, Frankie. Say something profound.*

Her heart was melting. She couldn't think! She took out her iCoffin and said the one thing she really, really wanted to say: "Sister Selfie!"

She handed the phone to Alivia, who studied the photo with great seriousness. Little sparks flicked from the electrodes on her neck. She smiled! She lurched forward and threw her arms around Frankie for a big hug. *Awwww!*

Science was one thing, but sisterhood was another. Just wait until her ghoulfriends met Alivia!

Chapter 15

What Monster Is This?

The ghouls had made a replica of Monster High for their float, and they were struggling to put the bell tower on the top of the school. They finally locked it into place and breathed a sigh of relief. Cleo, who was sitting off to the side, was checking something on her iCoffin.

"Can we get you anything, Cleo?" Clawdeen asked, panting and smoothing her hair back into place.

Cleo raised an eyebrow. "I know you're being sarcastic, but actually, since you asked, my iCoffin is about to die. Anyone have a charger?"

"You're supposed to be helping us with the float, mate." Lagoona was getting annoyed.

"I am helping," drawled Cleo. "I'm supervising."

"What was the last thing we did?" Draculaura asked.

"Fine," said Cleo grumpily. "I'll get to work."

She stormed over to the front of the platform near the engine area. "Say I'm not helping," she muttered to herself. "They're gonna get so much helping they'll say, 'Okay, Cleo, that's enough with the helping…'"

She stared at the engine. Beside it was a thick instruction manual. "'*How to build your parade float engine in nine hundred easy steps*,'" she read aloud. "I've got this." She tossed the book aside and began shoving engine parts into the compartment.

Cleo felt someone standing over her, watching. "Hey," she requested. "Can you hand me that U-shaped doodad over there, smaller version of Frankie?"

Alivia handed Cleo the metal part. Cleo went to take it from her, met the ghoul's eyes, and screamed at the top of her lungs. "Gah!"

Frankie rushed over. "Alivia, these are my friends. Ghouls, meet Alivia. My sister!"

"Your sister?" Draculaura was thrilled.

"Nice!" agreed Lagoona.

"Oh my ghoul, hello," Clawdeen welcomed her.

"So impressive, Frankie," said Lagoona admiringly. "You actually built a little sister?"

Frankie beamed. "Isn't she voltageous? And boy is she a spark off the old neck bolt."

Alivia, excited, was bouncing up and down on her

toes. "Hi, ghouls!" she squeaked. "How come your car has a big house on it?"

"Well, Alivia, this car is actually—" Draculaura stepped in.

"Uh-uh-uh!" interrupted Frankie. "We can figure this out, can't we Alivia? Using the scientific method." She didn't want to miss a single teaching opportunity. She was going to be the best big sister ever.

"First," Frankie continued, "let's form a hypothesis, a guess about the car that we'll try to prove with science. Do you have a guess, Alivia?"

Alivia bit her lip, thinking. "Um," she stalled for time. A big grin lit up her face. She pointed at Draculaura. "My guess is that she knows why there's a house on it and could just tell me."

"That's technically correct." Clawdeen laughed.

Alivia had wandered over and found Cleo's iCoffin. She was studying it. She snapped a selfie and looked at it, pleased. She took another one of herself with a different expression.

Frankie was telling the others about her plans. "We're going to stay up all night doing lab experiments, solving equations. And if we're feeling really adventurous, I have a few old clocks that we can take apart and put back together."

"*Oooh!* Can I come?" asked Cleo sarcastically.

"We're going to have so much science fun," Frankie continued, ignoring her. "Right, Alvia? Alivia?"

The ghoul was transfixed, snapping photos of herself next to the float. She was trying out all different kinds of poses. *Snap! Snap!* Cleo noticed and slid into the frame with her. Frankie reached over and took away the iCoffin. She set it down on the float.

"Such an inquisitive mind!" she said. "Just like her big sis. Come on, Alivia. I have our whole day planned out."

"Oh." Alivia was disappointed. "Can I see that one more time?" She pointed at the iCoffin.

Frankie forced a laugh. "Oh, Alivia, but there's so much more to see! Let's go! Science awaits!"

Clawdeen suppressed a smile. Frankie was about to find out that having siblings could be a lot of work.

Chapter 16

Have Yourself a Happy Little Howliday

Frankie pulled Alivia back to the lab. It was time to do a little real science together. Then Alivia would really understand how much fun it could be. She made sure Alivia put on her safety goggles—and then she took out two tiny test tubes. She poured a single drop of liquid from one to the other. A tiny puff of smoke appeared. Frankie grinned, pleased with herself. This was going to be so exciting for Alivia.

But Alivia just looked bored. She was staring out the window where the ghouls were working on their float. Cleo was taking photos of everyone. Alivia wished she could be taking photos too.

Frankie grabbed two bigger test tubes. Weird ingredients were already bubbling inside of them. She poured the whole mixture of one into the other. *Kaboom!* Now this was a reaction! Frankie looked eagerly to Alivia's face. Alivia tried to smile, but she couldn't hide her boredom. She just couldn't. She looked out the window again.

Frankie frowned. She brought a series of beakers and cylinders over to the table, along with a cable. This would get Alivia's attention. Frankie began shaking one of the beakers as hard as she could. She poured it into another beaker and began shaking it even harder. "Ta-da!" shouted Frankie as colors exploded. Smoke filled the room, and Frankie coughed. When it settled down, she realized that Alivia had found her phone. She was looking at all the photos.

Alivia smiled at Frankie and took another selfie.

Frankie was not defeated. "Okay, Alivia," she admitted. "So chemistry isn't your thing. No big. But if this doesn't get you excited about science, nothing will." She rummaged in a drawer and pulled out a potato. "I am going to teach you how to turn this into a battery!" she announced. She showed Alivia a battery.

"Why do we need to make a potato battery when you already have one right there?" asked Alivia innocently.

Frankie felt like Dracula when he was getting a question he wasn't prepared for. "I—well, because—" she stammered. "Because this battery doesn't use potato science?"

Alivia had wandered off and was hunting through a box of old junk. "Oh cool," she said. "Frankie, what's this?"

"That's a camera," said Frankie.

"Oh." Alivia was confused. "Where's the phone part?"

"They used to just be cameras," Frankie explained. "Weird, I know."

Alivia was fascinated. She blew the dust off the camera. "Can I try it out?" she asked.

"Sure." What else could Frankie say? "Go ahead."

"Voltageous!" Alivia was thrilled. At last she was excited about something. "Thanks, Frankie," she gushed, throwing her arms around her big sister and creator.

Frankie tried to smile. Somehow this wasn't what she'd imagined. But it wasn't all bad. Not at all.

Dracula teaches the Monster High students about human holidays.

Draculaura travels to Normie Town to see a human holiday.

Draculaura wants monsters to have their very own howliday!

The ghouls create All Monsters Day, a celebration of every kind of monster.

But Draculaura wants a big vampire family for the howliday. She decides to rescue the lost vampire princess, Fangelica Van Bat!

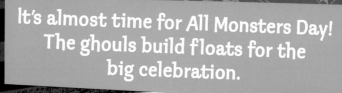

It's almost time for All Monsters Day!
The ghouls build floats for the
big celebration.

But Frankie can't concentrate. She wishes she had a little sister, too.

Frankie creates a sister just like her. Meet Alivia!

Clawdeen's little brothers are too excited to sleep before All Monsters Day! Clawdeen promises to get them in bed.

But first they have to win a snowball fight!

On All Monsters Day, Draculaura gives Fangelica a present—a picture of them together!

Fangelica flies to Normie Town to find a present for Draculaura.

A little Normie captures Fangelica!
Will the ghouls rescue her in time
for the celebration?

Chapter 17

Monsters Are Coming to Normie Town!

The float was almost finished! There was a replica of Monster High and the Mapalogue—and lots of monsters arriving for the first day of class.

"Fangtastic job, you ghouls," enthused Draculaura from beside the float. "This float is just about ready for the big howliday parade."

"All that's left," Clawdeen noted, "is to finish building..."

"The engine?" Cleo emerged from behind the engine panel, looking remarkably unruffled. She dusted her hands. "Taken care of," she said confidently as she climbed into the float.

Lagoona was stunned. "Cleo, you put together that whole engine by yourself?"

Cleo kicked back in the driver's seat, her feet up in the air. "Sure! It was easy. I can build engines in my sleep. In fact, I built one in my sleep last night.

I would show you, but that engine is long gone, driving down the open road. Because I built it so well, you see."

Clawdeen was skeptical. "Right."

Frankie arrived but seemed to barely notice the completed float. She was tossing a potato back and forth in her hands, and she looked distracted.

"Frankie, what's the matter?" asked Draculaura. "Where's Alivia?"

"Oh, she's off taking pictures or something." Frankie sighed.

"Sounds like your little sister's really taking a liking to photography," said Lagoona.

"Yeah, well…" Frankie did not seem happy. "What do you think allows the photons of light to react with the film emulsion in that camera?"

No one said anything. At last Clawdeen spoke up. "Potatoes?"

"Science!" exclaimed Frankie, exasperated.

"That was my second guess," Clawdeen said with a grin.

But Draculaura could tell what was the matter. "I'm sensing your day of fun-filled sister science didn't go the way you planned?"

"I don't get it!" Frankie said. "I triple-checked every equation from my own neck bolts. I just don't

understand why she's not like me."

"Alivia *is* like you, Frankie," Lagoona told her gently. "She's smart and independent and forming her own opinions and interests."

"Even if those interests aren't exactly the same as yours," added Draculaura. She looked over at Fangelica, busily working on decorations for the float.

Frankie sighed. "I guess I was just hoping we'd have something to bond over. You know, before the howliday."

"You see, Frankie," announced Cleo from the driver's seat, "the thing about family relationships…" She didn't realize that while she was lecturing everyone she had unknowingly kicked the brake release—and the float was rolling away. "And if you work at it long enough, all of a sudden you discover you're an expert. Why am I moving?"

"Cleo, the float is moving!" Clawdeen shouted. "Step on the brake!"

"Right! Which one's the brake?" Cleo was in a panic.

"Didn't you say you built the engine?" asked Draculaura.

"I say a lot of things!" cried Cleo.

Alivia was snapping photos of Fangelica's decorations when she saw her sister's moving float.

"Oh no," she cried. Without even thinking, she clambered up onto the float right next to her. It was Rayth and Deuce's rock-and-roll float. Alivia pushed past a guitar and got in the driver's seat. She turned on the engine and put her pedal to the gas.

"All right!" exclaimed Deuce from atop the float. "I guess we're rolling."

"Which means we gotta start rocking," Rayth said while strumming his bass.

Frankie was upset. Her sister didn't know how to drive! "Alivia!" she called. "Wait!"

The float careened down the hill in front of the school. "Hey," Alivia began. "I just realized I'm only a few hours old and don't know how to drive this thing. *Help!*"

A tiny set of hands appeared beside hers on the wheel! It was Fangelica. She'd followed Alivia onto the float. "How hard can this be?" she said. "I got this!" She steered expertly down the hill. She was small, but she wasn't born yesterday.

"Thank you!" said Alivia to her new friend.

The boys on the back of the float were rocking out. Skelly was wailing on the drums. Alivia was snapping photos of everything—the boys in the band, Fangelica driving the float, and everyone on the sidelines screaming.

Frankie had found the Mapalogue. Her little sister was in danger. *"Alivia. Exsto monstrum!"* she told it. An instant later, she had teleported onto the rock-and-roll float just as it careened over a bump—and the Mapalogue fell out of Frankie's hands.

"Watch where you're driving!" Frankie screeched.

"I am!" said Fangelica. "I'm trying to catch up to the other float."

Far in the distance, the other float of Monster High was headed right for Normie Town. This was terrible! "Oh my ghoul," whispered Frankie, alarmed. "We can't let the humans see *us*!"

"How close can you get us?" she asked Fangelica. "We have to stop that float!"

Fangelica's hands were tight on the steering wheel, and she was fierce and focused. She was a good driver. *Vroom!* She pressed her foot on the gas, and they zoomed up close to the other float.

Frankie knew what she had to do. She leaped from one moving float to another. Alivia was snapping photos like crazy. She thought Frankie was amazing!

Frankie grabbed the steering wheel from Cleo, but now she realized why the ghoul hadn't turned the float around. The wheel was locked. "We have to start the engine!" she told the mummy.

She turned the key, but nothing happened. She

opened up the engine compartment to see what was the matter—and everything was the matter. There was no engine, just a lot of random parts all in in a pile. "Cleo!" she screamed.

"Frankie, I'm going to be completely honest with you," Cleo confided. "Somebody must have sabotaged the perfectly good engine I built."

They were getting closer and closer to Normie Town. There was no time to lose. How quickly could she assemble an engine? She started piecing parts together.

Alivia was photographing it all from the other float while Fangelica steered expertly.

"That might work," said Frankie, "but there's no battery…"

But there was! She pulled the potato out of her pocket, jammed some screws and wires into it, and attached it with duct tape to the engine.

"Wow!" Alivia was impressed.

Frankie slammed the potato battery into the engine and turned the key.

Wrrr, wrr, wrr. Would it turn over?

"Come on," begged Frankie.

Wrr, wrr, wrr…VAROOM! The engine fired up. Sparks flew into the air. Electricity traveled into the float.

"Yes!" shouted Alivia.

The boys in the band played a string of power chords.

"Hang on!" shouted Frankie. With a screech, she whirled the float around on the road and headed back up the hill to Monster High. Fangelica whirled the other float around and followed her.

Phew! They had avoided disaster just in time.

Both floats chugged back to Monster High.

"What did you do?" Clawdeen asked Frankie.

"My sister saved the day!" Alivia jumped off the rock-and-roll float and ran over to Frankie. "With science! Can you teach me to do that?"

"I can." Frankie was touched, but she'd learned something too. "But only if you show me some of those action photos you took."

Alivia handed her the iCoffin, and Frankie swiped through the pictures. "These are really good," she complimented her. "Hey, I look kinda cool. Where'd you get all this talent?"

"Well…" Alivia blushed. "…you made me. So it obviously came from you!"

Meanwhile, Draculaura had found Fangelica. "Pretty fancy driving," she said to the little vampire.

"I used my bat sonar," confessed the ghoul. "When I couldn't see."

"I'm gonna have to try that!" said Draculaura.

"I think this is gonna be the best howliday ever!" Frankie announced.

But Rayth and Deuce weren't so sure. Something was the matter with their float. The engine was clanging and sputtering.

"Whoa," exclaimed Rayth. "That doesn't sound good."

Deuce put down his guitar. "I'm sure it's no big. Probably just need to make a few adjustments to the engine."

"You guys want me to take a look at it?" suggested Cleo.

"*No!*" screamed everyone.

Cleo shrugged. "Okay, yeah." Really, monsters so overreacted sometimes.

Chapter 18

Let It Snow!

"**F**angtastic job, everybody," complimented Draculaura. Monsters were decorating the main hall and rushing around as they had been for the past two days preparing for the howliday. "All Monsters' Day is tomorrow!"

Bonesy was pushing Skelly on a rolling platform. Skelly was standing absolutely still, but he was flickering and sparkling with holiday lights that had been strung from his skull to his feet bones. He was Monster High's very first holiday skeleton.

Gob was walking down the hallway deliberately touching each locker and leaving behind a blob of goo. Gil followed him and stuck festive spider and bat decorations to the sticky spots.

Abbey had abandoned her ice block and was focusing her talents on more popular Arctic decorations. "And now an ever-so-gentle dusting of howliday snow," she announced. She tossed a handful of mini-marshmallows into the air, waved her hand, and a few delicate flurries began to drift through the hall.

"That's wonderful!" exclaimed Lagoona. "But can you do a little more snow than that?"

Abbey tossed another handful of marshmallows into the air and again waved her hand. A few more flurries drifted down.

"Maybe just a little more," Frankie suggested.

Abbey tossed the whole bag of marshmallows into the air and waved her hand. *Whump.* A bitter wind blew down the hallway. A thick blanket of snow began to blizzard, covering everyone in a thick, cold layer of white.

"Perfect," announced Cleo.

In the art studio, Clawdeen's mom was working on special favors for the big day. Scraps of ribbon and paper were strewn about the room.

"Hey, Mom," said Clawdeen, coming into the room. "Brought you some tea." She held up a dog bowl–shaped mug with a handle. It was steaming hot.

"*Awww*, thank you, sweet pup," said her mom.

"How's it going with your howliday favors?" Clawdeen asked.

Her mother grinned. "Watch this."

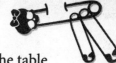

She set a little wrapped present down on the table in front of Clawdeen. She gave the shiny ribbon a little tug, and as she did so, the lid popped open and a bunch of colorful paper bats fluttered up into the air. They exploded like tiny fireworks, and confetti drifted down.

"Clawesome!" Clawdeen told her mom, clapping her hands delightedly.

"I'm going to make one for every single student here at the school," her mother told her.

"How many have you made so far?"

"Just that one," said Clawdeen's mom. "Probably shouldn't have used it up on that demonstration." She took a sip of tea, thinking. "Looks like I'm going to be up all night working on these.
I'll get back to it after I put your brothers to bed."

"Oh no, Mom. Let me take care of the werepups," Clawdeen suggested. "You've already got you paws full."

Her mom hesitated. "You think you can handle the pups' bedtime?"

"You don't think I can do it? Mom, I am, like, so responsible!"

"As responsible as you were with your iCoffin?"

Clawdeen blushed. Her phone was seriously cracked.

"Still, it would be a big help if you could get the werepups down," said her mother. "But if they give you any trouble, just let me know."

"Mom, please. When you see how fast I get the boys to go to bed, you are gonna say, 'Clawdeen, you are the queen of responsible. Have a new iCoffin.'"

Her mom laughed. So that was the plan. "You know what? You get those boys to bed, and I'll get new iCoffins for you and all your friends."

Wow! Clawdeen had never seen her mother so generous. The howliday spirit was making everyone a little happier and a lot more giving. Now all she had to do was get her brothers to bed on time before the big day. How hard could that be?

Chapter 19

The Night Before All Monsters' Day

Clawdeen got the pups into their bunk beds with the promise of a story. "And then the brave little werepup looked up at the full moon and said, '*HOWWWWWWWWWWL!*'"

"*Ah-hoooooooowwwwwlll,*" echoed the pups in unison.

Clawdeen shut her book. "The end," she announced. "Time to go to sleep. But when you wake up, it'll finally be All Monsters' Day."

The werepups wagged their tails happily and barked.

"First thing in the morning, we're gonna celebrate with a big howliday parade. Then we'll exchange presents and sing monster carols. And then…" Her voice trailed off. One of the pups was missing. His bed was empty. "Where's Barker?"

Far away, down the hall, she heard the sound

of claws on the floorboards and someone quietly yipping. There was Barker at the end of the hall, running happily in circles.

"All right, all right," Clawdeen told him. "I know you're excited about the howliday, but it's time for bed. Let's go."

She led Barker back to the bunkroom by his collar—but now all the other pups were out of bed and gone. Where could they be?

"Oh boy," Clawdeen said with a sigh. This was not going to be as easy as she thought. She raced out of the room and down the staircase looking for them.

Her mother noticed her hurrying past the art studio. "Clawdeen?" she called. "Is everything okay? Do you need help with the boys?"

"Nope! Everything's great, Mom!" she responded with false cheerfulness. "I do not need help."

A few seconds later, Clawdeen burst into Draculaura's bedroom where her friends were fanging out. "I need help!" she gasped.

Draculaura rushed over to her friend. "What's the matter, Clawdeen?"

"Is it a lost monster mission?" asked Frankie.

"A natural disaster?" Cleo said, worried.

"Do we have to save the world from certain doom?" wondered Lagoona.

Clawdeen panted, trying to catch her breath. "I need help putting my kid brothers to bed." The ghouls stared at her, dumbstruck.

Lagoona gulped. "You sure we can't just save the world from certain doom?"

"We get new iCoffins if we can do it," Clawdeen explained.

Still, the ghouls were unsure. "Saving the world from certain doom sounds easier," said Frankie.

Clawdeen had the Mapalogue. *"Barker. Exsto monstrum,"* she intoned. The next moment she was in the main hallway, and Barker was scampering right toward her. She grabbed him by the paw and marched him back to the bunkroom.

Lagoona was searching the lockers and, sure enough, a werepup popped out of the second one she opened. Cleo opened another locker, and a whole pack of pups poured out of it, barking and licking her face.

"Got more than one," she said as she herded them all upstairs.

Clawdeen counted the pups. *"Pawlie. Exsto monstrum,"* she told the Mapalogue.

That's how she found herself hanging from the chandelier in the main hall. Pawlie grinned at her. Using the Mapalogue, she got him to bed as well.

Draculaura and Frankie were trying a different strategy. They'd settled in the library with a bowl of puppy treats. It didn't take long for three pups to show up and to begin snacking.

"Now!" said Frankie.

Draculaura took a pair of jumper cables and clamped them to Frankie's neck bolts. A fence of electricity surrounded the pups, and it was easy to herd them upstairs. Meanwhile, Clawdeen had used the Mapalogue one last time to find the last pup… just as he was about to head into the art studio and surprise Clawdeen's mom.

Clawdeen counted the pups in their bunks. None was missing. At last. They had done it! "All right," she said. "That's all of them. Now. It is time for bed. Good night." She clicked off the light. But as she tiptoed out of the room, she heard something. She flicked the lights back on, and it was just what she suspected. All the pups were out of their beds again.

"Technically, we did get them into bed," said Cleo, defeated. "Did your mom say anything about them having to stay in bed?"

Where had they gone this time?

Chapter 20

A Winter Wonderland of Werepups

The ghouls followed the sound of barking to the main hall, where the puppies were all romping together in the winter wonderland Abbey had created. They were rolling in the snow to make snow monsters.

"Look at them." Draculaura laughed. "I think they're just too excited about the howliday to go to sleep."

Clawdeen was less amused. "Playtime is over," she told them.

A snowball flew through the air, and Clawdeen dodged it. Another came right toward her face, and she caught it one-handed.

"Okay," she said, her eyes narrowing. "You boys want to play in the snow? Let's play in the snow. But here's the deal. If you can beat me and the ghouls at a snowball fight, then you can stay up as late as you want."

The werepups wagged their tails, excited. Yes! That's what they wanted to do!

"But," Clawdeen continued, calmly forming one snowball after another and piling them up beside her, "if we win—which we will—you go right to bed. Dodgeball rules. You get hit, you're out. Last team standing wins. Deal?"

She extended her hand, and Barker shook it. Deal! He dashed to join his brothers. Let the snowball fight begin.

"Are you sure about this, mate?" Lagoona asked, worried.

"Yeah," Frankie agreed, looking over at the werepups. "We're kind of outnumbered."

"Please," scoffed Clawdeen. "We've traveled the world finding monsters. We've climbed a mountain. We've surfed down the side of a volcano! How tough can a few werepups be?"

Snowballs began flying through the air. The ghouls retreated behind a column as fast as they could.

"We need a plan," said Frankie.

"I've got a plan," Cleo proclaimed. With a wild war cry, she charged toward the pups hurling snowballs. *Zowie! Kaboom! Plop.* She was covered from head to toe in snow. "Yeah, I'm out," she said with a sigh. "Don't do my plan."

Clawdeen was thinking. "All right, Frankie, you see if you can engineer some kind of home base out of snow. Lagoona, you flank left. I'll go right. And Draculaura, take the sky!"

"And what about me?" questioned a small voice. It was Fangelica.

"I thought you were asleep," said Draculaura.

"I was trying to fall asleep, but I heard all of the noise, and I wanted to see what all of the excitement was about!"

"Me too!" It was Alivia, grinning. She hurried over to Frankie.

"Well, at least we've got better numbers on our side," noted Clawdeen.

"And more monsters to put to bed," Draculaura thought aloud.

"You ghouls ready?" asked Clawdeen.

"Ready!"

"Operation Snowball begins!" Clawdeen shouted.

Frankie and Alivia began constructing a snow fort. Draculaura and Fangelica turned into bats and swooped through the air. They swerved and twisted, avoiding snowballs. They dove toward the pups.

"Haha! You've got to do better than that!" exclaimed Draculaura. She swooped down in a nose dive, Fangelica beside her. They skimmed the surface of the snow and aimed themselves like torpedoes right at the pups.

"Incoming!" whooped Fangelica. She was having a blast.

Draculaura dropped two snowballs, one right after the other, onto the furry heads of two pups.

"And you're out!" called Fangelica.

A werepup had spotted Lagoona and threw an armful of snowballs in her direction. But Lagoona swung open a locker door at the last moment like a shield. The snowballs ricocheted off the door and hit the pup instead!

Lagoona looked at the door. *Hmmm.* She had an idea. She pulled it off its hinges and threw it down in front of her. Surfing and snowboarding weren't that different, and it was time to catch some drifts! She sprayed snow as she careened toward the pups. She hit a snowbank and ramped into the air, unleashing handfuls of snowballs on the pups' heads as she flew over them.

Clawdeen had changed into a wolf and was bounding across the snow, dodging balls.

Frankie had finished constructing a gigantic snow fortress while Alivia snapped photos of the epic snowball fight.

"It's not much, but it should do the job," said Frankie.

"Fall back!" ordered Lagoona to the others.

The ghouls zoomed into the fort. *Thunk. Thunk. Thunk.* Balls rebounded off the walls.

"You ghouls are doing clawesome!" complimented Frankie. "But we're not out of this yet."

"I am." Cleo was sitting in a corner tapping on her phone. "I am out of this."

"As long as we can keep the werepups out of this fort, victory—and possibly new iCoffins—are as good as ours."

Boom! The werepups were using Barker like a battering ram to break down the walls of the snow fort.

"Wow," commented Lagoona. "They really don't want to go to bed."

Outside the fort, the pups had removed some locker doors and put them over mounds of snow like seesaws. One pup sat on one side, and on the other, a werepup jumped as hard as he could, sending his brother flying over the snow wall. The werepups, snowballs in their paws, landed beside the ghouls.

"*Ah!*" screamed Lagoona, laughing. "We've been breached!"

Twap! Twap! Twap! A trio of snowballs hit Draculaura. She was out.

Barker burst through the snow wall, barking happily.

"The fort has been compromised," cried Frankie. "Everybody, out!"

Fangelica pulled a lever, and an ice slide dropped down from the top of the fort to the ground.

"Clawesome!" said Clawdeen. The ghouls were about to slide down it, one after the other. But Draculaura stopped Clawdeen.

"Time to put this mission to bed," Draculaura announced. She tossed Clawdeen a snowball. Together they slid down side by side.

Snowballs were flying, the pups were barking and racing in circles, and the ghouls were hurling snowballs all around them. Down went a pup! Down went another. A snowball plopped into Lagoona. Frankie was out a moment later.

A snowball hit Alivia's camera. "Hey! No fair!" she shouted. "I'm taking photos of everyone for our howliday album!"

Clawdeen was racing this way and that way. She dove sideways and took down a line of werepups one after the other.

Two werepups lowered their heads in front of her.

"If my calculations are correct," said Frankie, "those are the last two."

"So if Clawdeen can get them out, we win!" Draculaura was excited.

"*Woo-hooo!*" cheered Lagoona.

Cleo yawned and stood up. "Hey, Clawdeen, time to put this mission to bed."

"Um, Draculaura already said that," answered Clawdeen without taking her eyes off the pups.

Cleo was surprised. "She did?"

"*Mmm,*" said Draculaura.

"All cool, like in an action movie?" Cleo asked.

"Yep," explained Clawdeen.

"Oh." Cleo was confused. "Because we're, like, trying to get the werepups to go to bed, so putting the mission to bed is like a—"

"Yeah, yeah," interrupted Clawdeen. "We got it."

"Okay," answered Cleo, and she sat down again.

The pups were studying Clawdeen, waiting to make their next moves. It was a standoff. The pups' tongues were out, and they were panting. Clawdeen had a snowball in each hand. She dropped to her knees. The pups let their last snowballs fly. Clawdeen slid between them and gently tapped each one on the head.

"Bedtime," she said.

Everyone cheered. The pups barked and chased one another in circles. Their eyes were beginning to droop.

Chapter 21

A Howliday Tradition

Clawdeen breathed a sigh of relief. She'd done the impossible, and now it was time to put these pups to bed—and get her brand-new iCoffin.

Splat! A snowball dropped from above right on her head. Huh? She looked up—and there, hanging from the chandelier, was Barker. He waved a paw, grinning.

Frankie was counting pups. "Wait a minute. Oh no, I was wrong. There's still one werepup in the game. We just lost."

"Awooo!" howled the pups. *"Awooo!"*

Clawdeen sighed, defeated. "All right, boys. A deal's a deal. You can stay up as late as you want."

"On the bright side," noted Cleo, "I got a lot of howliday shopping done while you ghouls were playing." She waved her iCoffin happily.

Draculaura patted Cleo on the back. "Sorry, Clawdeen. The important thing is we all tried our best."

"I guess." Clawdeen sighed. "But now I have to tell my mom I'm not responsible enough to get the boys to go to sleep. Good-bye, new iCoffin."

Lagoona giggled. "Maybe not, mate. Look."

The werepups weren't running anymore. They were tottering in place, their eyes barely open. Barker yawned. A couple of the pups curled up in the snow and fell asleep.

Very quietly, the ghouls scooped up the werepups and tucked each into bed. One of the pups began to snore. Clawdeen tiptoed out of the room.

Her mom was out in the hallway. She peeked into the bunkroom. "I'm impressed, Clawdeen," she said with a smile. "You actually got the werepups to sleep?"

"Sure did," said Clawdeen, as if it had been nothing.

"I'm sorry I doubted you," her mother apologized. "Sounds like I know a few ghouls that might be getting new iCoffins for All Monsters' Day!"

The ghouls would have cheered, but the last thing they wanted to do was wake up the pups again. Draculaura noticed Fangelica was yawning. It was time for them to go to bed too.

The ghouls all brought their sleeping bags into Draculaura's room.

"Do you always have a sleepover on All Monsters' Day Eve?" Alivia asked Frankie.

Frankie turned to her little sister. "I think we will. Let's make it a tradition."

"You know," said Draculaura, "that snowball fight was actually kind of fun."

"It really was!" gushed Fangelica. "Let's make that a tradition too."

"That was a great day!" Lagoona told her.

Cleo snuggled into her sleeping bag. "Well, we have a big day ahead of us tomorrow, so I'm going to make like a werepup and get some sleep."

The ghouls sighed and stretched out. Draculaura turned off the light. Webby was asleep in a hammock hung from his web. Fangelica curled up beside her, her eyes shut.

"*Cock-a-doodle-doo!*" Somewhere a rooster was crowing.

The ghouls sat up, rubbing their eyes, confused.

"Is it morning already?" asked Clawdeen.

Frankie got out of her sleeping bag and peeked through the curtains. The sun was coming up! "That snowball fight kept us up the entire night!"

"Oh," moaned Lagoona, "I'm going to be exhausted all day...."

"Wait a minute," Draculaura said excitedly. "Do you know what this means? All Monsters' Day! It's finally here!"

Cleo sat up and opened her eyes wide. "Draculaura's right! Who has time to be tired? Come on, ghouls!"

But no one moved. They were too exhausted.

Clawdeen's eyes were drooping. Draculaura was lying back down.

"Maybe we snooze for five minutes," said Cleo with a yawn.

And they all fell fast asleep.

Chapter 22

A Holly Jolly Howliday

The werepups woke up barking with excitement, and the ghouls were up moments later, rubbing their tired eyes. Everyone was excited. The spirit of the howlidays filled them all.

"It's here!" Alivia whispered to Frankie.

"Happy Howlidays!" exclaimed Fangelica.

Snow was falling as they descended the stairs. There were presents in front of each of their lockers. Deuce was stirring a big steaming pot over the fire.

"Here's my contribution to tonight's howliday meal. Ghoulillabaise à la Deuce!" Deuce offered Gob a taste, and Gob swallowed the whole ladle. He gave Deuce the thumbs-up. Yummy!

But Deuce still thought it needed a little something else. "More dragon ghost chili powder," he muttered to himself.

Bonesy was already opening up one of his presents.

It was Skelly's skull! Bonesy gave him a big hug. Best present ever!

Fangelica was filled with wonder as she looked around the hall at all the happy students sharing this special day together. She remembered her lonely castle back in Transylvania. She was so lucky Draculaura had come looking for her! Just being here was the best present of all.

A bat fluttered down before her, holding a gift.

"Happy Howliday," said Draculaura, transforming back into herself.

"What's this?" Fangelica wondered out loud

Draculaura shrugged. "Oh, just a little something. Nothing big."

Very carefully, Fangelica untied the ribbon and removed the wrapping paper. She peeked inside the box and pulled out a picture frame.

"Ta-da!" announced Draculaura. "It's a picture of you and me! Alivia took it."

Neither ghoul was actually in the photo, but their outfits were recognizable. "I mean, you can't see us," Draculaura explained. "Because vampires don't show up in pictures. But we're there. Trust me."

Fangelica clutched the photo happily. She beamed at Draculaura, tears welling up in her eyes. "Oh, Draculaura, it's fangtastic! But I didn't get you anything. I didn't know…"

"You do not have to get me a thing," Draculaura reassured the little ghoul. "Just promise to save me a seat next to you for the big howliday dinner. But it's almost time for the parade! See you there?"

Fangelica nodded. But she seemed concerned. She looked at the picture again, frowning. But a huge explosion interrupted her thoughts.

Deuce was burned to a crisp, and Gob had turned all black and charred.

"Too much chili powder?" gasped Deuce.

Gob nodded, smoke coming off his body.

Luckily, Deuce had the whole rest of the day to get it right. Now it was time for the parade. Deuce and Gob rushed outside with the rest of the monsters.

Only Fangelica lagged behind. There was something she needed to do.

Chapter 23

Last-Minute Howliday Shopping

Engines were starting, and the floats were beginning to roll. The parade was about to begin. Monsters cheered and shouted. The werepups howled happily.

Deuce was rocking on his bass. Rayth and Bonesy were strumming their guitars. Skelly was keening with a high-pitched screech. The crowd cheered and sang along.

Abbey's float was covered in snow, and she stood at the center of it, dressed as an ice queen with a crown. Barker saw the snow and raced toward the float to make snowballs, but Abbey zapped him with an icicle and stopped him in his tracks.

The musical ghouls—Catty Nori, Ari Hauntington, and Operetta—were singing howliday songs in matching outfits and, again, the crowd joined in and sang along.

The last float was the ghouls' tribute to Monster High. There was the high school, the Mapalogue, the monsters headed to class. The ghouls waved at their classmates. Cleo held up her hand like a queen greeting her subjects.

"This parade is happening so fast," she complained. "When we get to the end, what do you say we turn the float around and go back past the school for a victory lap?"

Frankie peered into the crowd and saw Alivia snapping photos with her camera. "Alivia!" she called. "Over here!"

"Hey, sis!" called the little ghoul.

Draculaura was also looking into the crowd and frowning. Lagoona noticed that she seemed upset. "Something wrong, mate?" she asked.

"I don't see Fangelica," Draculaura said, worried. "She said she'd be here."

"That's strange," Lagoona noted. "Fangelica was really excited about the parade."

Draculaura nodded. "I know. Can the ghouls help me look for her when the parade is over?"

"Of course," agreed Lagoona. She looked around, surprised by something. "Hey, are we turning around?"

Cleo was in the driver's seat of the float. Her foot was on the gas, and she was turning the wheel hard to spin the float around in the other direction. "Victory lap!" she shouted.

The ghouls all cheered—except Draculaura. Something far in the distance had caught her eye. Was it a bat? Was it Fangelica? Where was she going? With a pang, Draculaura thought that maybe she was headed back to Transylvania. What would she do without her?

Fangelica fluttered her wings high above Normie Town. She was muttering to herself, "Gotta find her a present. Gotta find her a good present." But what was that present? How could she show Draculaura how much she meant to her? She swooped down toward the ground.

Before her was an empty stretch of road. Fangelica looked around, frustrated. "Where am I, anyway?" she wondered out loud. Was she lost? She had a sneaking suspicion that she might be. But before she could decide if she was or not, a butterfly net fell around her.

"Gotcha!" called a voice.

Fangelica had just been captured—by a little human girl.

Chapter 24

How the Girl Stole the Vampires

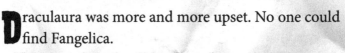

Draculaura was more and more upset. No one could find Fangelica.

"She wasn't in the Creepateria," reported Cleo.

"She wasn't in the art classroom, either," Clawdeen informed her.

Frankie appeared. "I checked the science lab. Nothing."

Lagoona's eyes narrowed, noticing something. "Frankie," she scolded. "Did you do science while you were in the lab?"

"What? No!" responded Frankie defensively.

"Show us your hands," ordered Cleo.

Busted! Frankie held out her hands, and they were covered in chalk dust. "It was one equation," she explained. "And I didn't even finish solving it!"

Draculaura was thinking. "It's time to get the Mapalogue. But I don't want my dad or anyone to

worry about us and ruin their howliday. Clawdeen
and Cleo, you come with me to lend a helping hand.
Frankie and Lagoona, you stay here and cover for us
until we get back with Fangelica."

Draculaura, Cleo, and Clawdeen placed their hands
on the Mapalogue and disappeared.

Frankie had a faraway look in her eyes.

"Still thinking about that equation, aren't you?"
questioned Lagoona.

"I'm almost done! I promise," Frankie explained.

Lagoona took her by the arm. They had to keep
an eye on things. No one could know that the littlest
ghoul was missing.

Meanwhile, Draculaura and her ghouls had teleported. Draculaura, still holding the Mapalogue, looked around. Where were they? Where had it taken them? She'd been sure they were headed to Transylvania, but they didn't see mountains and castles—just ordinary human houses. "Oh my ghoul," recognized Draculaura. "I know this house. We're in Normie Town! This is where I watched the humans celebrate their holiday."

"But where is Fangelica?" asked Clawdeen, worried.

They listened. Far above them, they heard an unmistakable sound—the flutter of bat wings.

"I'll be right back," announced Draculaura, immediately transforming herself into a bat. She flapped her wings and headed toward an upstairs window.

"I hope she finds her fast," Clawdeen whispered to Cleo. "I'm really getting hungry."

"Hey," grinned Cleo. "Check it out. I snuck some dinner rolls from the Creepateria into my purse!"

Clawdeen was shocked. "Those are for the howliday dinner! We're not supposed to eat those until we're all together."

But Cleo wasn't paying any attention. She was already devouring one of the rolls. "So you want one or what?" she asked Clawdeen between mouthfuls.

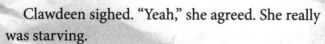

Clawdeen sighed. "Yeah," she agreed. She really was starving.

Draculaura flew into the open window of the house and screamed. A snarling monster guarded the way. Or rather, a snarling monster toy. Draculaura breathed a sigh of relief as she looked around the bedroom. It was filled with monsters, all kinds of monsters— ghouls and ghosties, bats and spiders, mummies and wraiths.

"Wow," Draculaura whispered. "This Normie girl is really into us!"

"Draculaura?" It was Fangelica! She was still a bat— and hanging upside down inside an iron birdcage on a shelf. She was trapped.

"Fangelica!" Draculaura cried. This was terrible. She flew directly toward the cage and tried to open it with her bat feet. She didn't dare change into her monster self. She struggled to unlock it, but she couldn't. "It's stuck."

Fangelica could hear footsteps coming up the stairs. "You've got to hide," she urged Draculaura. "She's coming!"

"Batty?" called a voice. It was the human girl.

Draculaura tugged on the latch to the cage one more time. But it was no use. She flapped her wings and looked for a place to hide, but the room was so bright. The footsteps were getting closer. "I'll be back. You just hang on right there."

"Funny," Fangelica said with a grimace.

Draculaura grinned. "I thought so." She flew toward the window as fast as she could—but it was too late. The window was slammed shut—and a little human girl was standing in front of it. *Splat!* Draculaura hit the glass and slid down to the floor.

Outside, Clawdeen and Cleo heard the noise and looked up. They stopped munching on their rolls. Uh-oh. They swallowed, worried. Something was wrong. They could tell. Something was very wrong.

Chapter 25

Here Comes Mr. Dracula

Back at Monster High, Lagoona and Frankie were hanging out in the hallway, trying to look as natural and festive as they could—all while spotting any potential problems. When they saw Dracula heading toward them, they turned around and tried to slip into a classroom. But he had seen them.

"Ah!" he called. "Frankie! Lagoona! I've been looking all over for Draculaura. I wanted to give her this howliday present." He held up an object that he was clearly very proud of—and which was clearly homemade. Craft sticks covered in stickers were glued to a tin can. "It's a…a…well, I'm not sure what it is. But I made it myself."

"You don't say," commented Lagoona, trying to keep from snickering.

"So, do you know where Draculaura is?" Dracula asked again.

"Yes!" said both ghouls together.

"Excellent! Can you tell me?"

"No," they both answered at the same time.

Dracula looked at them, confused. "You can't tell me where she is?"

Lagoona and Frankie shook their heads.

"It would spoil the surprise!" blurted Lagoona.

"Right!" agreed Frankie. "The howliday surprise. Your howliday present."

Dracula smiled, showing his fangs. "Ah!" he said, pleased. An instant later his face fell. "It's not one of those silly necktie-of-the-month subscriptions, is it?"

"No, no, no!" Frankie reassured him.

"Of course not," added Lagoona.

Unexpectedly, Dracula looked disappointed. "Oh."

"I mean yes," Frankie covered. She wanted to keep him happy so he wouldn't go looking for Draculaura.

Lagoona picked up on her plan. "That's totally what it is! You guessed!"

"Wonderful!" enthused Dracula. "As long as she's not late for howliday dinner. I can't wait to see the look on her face when she sees…well, whatever this is."

He looked at his craft-stick creation happily. It had really come out even better than he had planned. Draculaura was going to love it. He just knew.

Lagoona and Frankie couldn't even breathe until he had turned the corner away from them.

Now to go research necktie-of-the-month clubs for their friend. She was going to have to put in an order for a subscription as soon as she got back. Whenever that was.

Chapter 26

Home for the Howlidays

Draculaura was imprisoned in the cage with Fangelica. Both bats were hanging upside down. They didn't dare talk to each other, not in front of the human girl. She was admiring her new pets.

"I can't believe I have two bats," she said. "This is gonna be so great. I'm gonna call you Batarina," she said to Fangelica, "and you Flappy," she told Draculaura.

"Honey, dinner!" called a voice.

"Coming," answered the girl.

As soon as she was out of the room, Draculaura turned to Fangelica. "Batarina is a lot prettier than Flappy," she said, trying to cheer her up. Fangelica force a smile, but she was miserable. "Don't worry, we'll get out of here," Draculaura reassured her.

"Oh, I know we will," said Fangelica. "I just feel bad. It's my fault we got into this mess."

"What were you doing in Normie Town, anyway?" asked Draculaura.

"I got lost," Fangelica told her. "I wanted to find you the perfect howliday present."

"Fangelica!" Draculaura sighed. "I told you, you didn't have to get me anything!"

"I know. But I wanted to get you something really special. Because you're like a big sister to me."

Tears welled up in Draculaura's eyes. "You're not like a sister to me," she confided. "As far as I'm concerned, we are sisters." She hugged Fangelica. "And that is the best present I could ever get. Happy howlidays, little sister."

"Happy howlidays...Flappy!"

The ghouls shared a giggle but fell silent when they heard a scratching noise at the window pane.

Clawdeen's manicured red fingernails were just visible below the window sill. Slowly, with great effort, she pulled herself up to look into the room. Or rather, Cleo pulled her up. She had used one of her mummy bandages as a belay rope, hurling it over the awning of the house and then hauling Clawdeen up to the second floor.

"Don't worry, ghouls," Clawdeen called to them, now dangling in front of the window. "We'll get you out of there in two shakes of a werewolf's tail."

Clawdeen tugged at the window to open it, but it was locked. "C'mon," she urged. She pulled; she tugged; she fell backward and plummeted to the ground. As Clawdeen went down, Cleo flew up.

"Ahhh!" screamed Cleo. "Hi, ghouls!" she said before disappearing.

Both ghouls landed on the ground, and the mummy bandages fell in a heap on their heads.

"Well, that didn't work." Cleo sighed.

"We have to figure out some way to get into that room," Clawdeen said.

Cleo shrugged. "Yeah, but how? It's not like we can just walk up to the front door and ring the doorbell."

But maybe they could. Cleo had just given Clawdeen an excellent idea!

Chapter 27

They'll Be Back Again Someday!

Ding-dong! Cleo was ringing the doorbell of the house in Normie Town. She'd wrapped her bandages around her head like a turban, and she was wearing sunglasses so she looked like an old lady. She had a leash in her hand, and at the end of it was Clawdeen, changed into a wolf.

When the door opened, Cleo began her best grandma impressions. "Hello! My, um, doggie needs to use your bathroom," she said. "Can we come in?"

The startled family let Cleo and Clawdeen into their house, and they went up the stairs and searched for their ghoulfriends in an instant. They shut the door behind them when they went into the bedroom. Just like Draculaura, they were amazed by all the monster stuff. Cleo pulled the bandages from around her face.

"Wow," exclaimed Clawdeen, looking around.

"Look at all this creeperific monster stuff."

Cleo held up a mummy doll. "Imagine if one of these was a little me."

Clawdeen didn't waste any more time and opened the cage. Draculaura and Fangelica changed back to normal the moment they were free and stretched.

"You ghouls okay?" Clawdeen asked.

"We're fine," Draculaura told her. "The Normie girl was actually very sweet to us."

Fangelica nodded in agreement. "I feel kinda bad we have to leave without saying good-bye."

"It's too bad more humans aren't as into monsters as she is," said Clawdeen thoughtfully. "Then maybe we wouldn't have to keep hiding."

They all startled. They could hear footsteps on the stairs. There was no time to lose.

"She's coming back," Draculaura told the others. "Let's make with the Mapalogue and go!"

Clawdeen turned it on. The ghouls all put their hands on it.

"Monster High. Exsto—" she began but stopped when she saw that Cleo still had the mummy doll in her hands.

"Okay, okay, I'll put it back," Cleo said with a sigh.

"Monster High. Exsto monstrum!" finished Clawdeen.

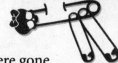

In the nick of time, they teleported and were gone.

Or almost. Because the little girl had heard, well, something. She looked around. Where had the old lady with the enormous doggie gone? Where were her bats?

"Hello?" she called. *"Hmmm."*

The little girl noticed a swirl of shimmering energy in the center of the room. What could that possibly be? The little girl reached her hand out to touch it.

And a moment later, she was gone.

Chapter 28

The Miracle at Monster High

The howliday meal was about to begin. The table was piled high with serving dishes, and students were beginning to take their seats and put their napkins on their laps.

"Is it time for the big meal yet?" asked Abbey.

"When can we eat?" wondered Deuce.

Gob devoured his napkin and then his plate and then his utensils

"Mr. Dracula," Rayth called out to the headmaster. "Can we eat yet? I'm *sooooo* hungry!"

"We all are," Deuce added. "Look at Bonesy and Skelly. They're nothing but bones and bones."

Dracula shook his head. "No, we cannot start eating until Draculaura and her ghoulfriends get here." His eyes fell on Gob. "Hey!" he reprimanded him. "I saw that."

Gob had put an entire serving dish of food into

his belly. Embarrassed, he pulled it out and put it back on the table, although now, of course, it was completely covered in sticky goo.

Dracula walked over to Frankie and Lagoona, who were looking around anxiously.

"Is there something you're not telling me?"

The ghouls exchanged guilty glances.

"Um—er—" Frankie stuttered.

"Well..." began Lagoona, stalling.

"Where are Draculaura and the ghouls?" Mr. Dracula asked sternly. Something was definitely up.

Frankie and Lagoona didn't know what to do. They didn't have any other possible covers. They were just about to open their mouths to confess when, with a flash, the ghouls appeared in the room!

"There they are!" shouted Frankie, relieved.

"Yep," Lagoona added. "Right there."

Dracula clapped his hands, delighted. "Ah, good! Now that everyone is here we can start the howliday dinner!"

The students cheered, and the ghouls rushed to take their seats.

"Hey, Dad, sorry we're late," Draculaura apologized.

"I'm just happy you're here," responded her father. "Can't spend the first monster howliday without my daughter."

Draculaura took Fangelica's hand and brought the little ghoul over to her father. "Oh, Dad," she began, "Fangelica and I decided we're sisters, so, technically, you have two daughters now."

Fangelica grinned happily. "Hi, Dad!" she said.

"Oh well, in that case…" Dracula was surprised. "I—wait a minute—I mean…"

The little vampire ghoul was looking up at him, her tiny fangs pressed against her lips. She looked just like Draculaura when she was only seven hundred years old. Dracula smiled warmly at her and patted her on the head. "I mean to say that I think this is fangtastic!"

Fangelica threw herself into his arms and hugged him tight. Draculaura joined the group hug too.

Alivia, who was sitting next to Frankie, reached out

and squeezed her hand. "I'm glad you made me your sister too."

"All right, everyone," Draculaura announced. "Happy All Monsters' Day!"

"Happy All Monsters' Day!" shouted all the monsters together.

Food was passed. Jokes and stories were told. Dracula made a speech that was just a little too long. The puppies forgot their manners and got pie all over their whiskers. Gob got enough to eat for once.

Off in a corner, Fangelica was teaching Alivia the vampire handshake. "First, you turn your fingers into fangs," she explained.

"Looks like things are going great for our new little ghouls," Frankie noted happily.

"Look at her smiling fang to fang," said Lagoona, pointing at Fangelica. "I keep thinking of how serious and unhappy she looked in that portrait at the castle. Now look at her."

Draculaura beamed at her little sister. "I can't thank you ghouls enough for helping me find her. I couldn't have done it without you."

"You know you can always count on us," said Clawdeen.

"Do you really mean that?" Draculaura asked. "Because finding Fangelica has got me thinking. There must be thousands of lost monsters in hiding out there, just waiting to be found. They're lonely and they need friends and they need family. They probably don't even know about howlidays."

"That's just terrible," agreed Lagoona.

"I want to find them all," announced Draculaura. "That's my All Monsters' Day resolution. I want to find all the sad and lost little monsters out there and let them know they've got a home. And if I'm going to find them all, I'm going to need all the help I can get."

Lagoona grinned. "Well, you've got to admit, we make a pretty creeperific team."

"We're, like, professional monster finders," said Cleo. "We should have a name and a theme song. Oh, and cool action poses. And, yes, a Sphinx. The one thing missing right now is a Sphinx."

"Maybe we should just start with the name," suggested Clawdeen. "Any ideas?" She looked around the table at the other ghouls.

Draculaura was quiet for a moment, and then inspiration struck. "How about the Ghoul Squad?"

"The Ghoul Squad," repeated Clawdeen, smiling.

"I like it!" said Clawdeen.

"Me too," said Frankie.

"It's not bad," Cleo admitted. "But we really need a theme song, and—I'm just putting it out there—a Sphinx logo."

The ghouls burst out laughing.

"Time for dessert, I think," suggested Draculaura, changing the subject.

"You know, Draculaura, this counts as a successful first monster howliday," Frankie said, looking around the room. Abbey was explaining to Operetta how she'd made her ice cream. Bonesy and Skelly were teasing each other. Dracula was handing a present to Clawdeen's mom. She opened it and inside of the box was a can covered in craft sticks, just like the one he'd made for Draculaura. She seemed to genuinely like it.

Clawdeen was thinking about something else. "I've gotta say that seeing that little Normie girl's room really gave me hope for the future. We all got along with one another—maybe someday they'll learn to get along with us."

"You should have seen it," Cleo told Frankie and Lagoona. "Monster stuff everywhere. Bats and ghost toys and the prettiest little mummy doll you have ever seen."

Draculaura laughed. "Little does she know, she lives right around the corner from a whole school of monsters. Can you imagine the look on her face if that little human girl could see us all right now?"

"You think she would look something like that?" Cleo pointed across the room.

A human face was peeking from behind the heavy

curtains. Her eyes wide and her face awestruck, she was watching the monsters. A little leftover glow from teleporting clung to her hair.

The monsters' mouths fell open. Uh-oh.

The little girl grinned. She couldn't wait to tell her parents. She always knew monsters were real!